FIRST PEOPLES

SHAWNEE

VALERIE BODDEN

CREATIVE EDUCATION ✕ CREATIVE PAPERBACKS

Published by Creative Education and Creative Paperbacks
P.O. Box 227, Mankato, Minnesota 56002
Creative Education and Creative Paperbacks are imprints of
The Creative Company
www.thecreativecompany.us

Design by Christine Vanderbeek
Production by Colin O'Dea
Art direction by Rita Marshall
Printed in the United States of America

Photographs by Bridgeman Art Library (Troiani, Don [b. 1949]), Creative Commons Wikimedia (Bowen, John T./SMU Central University Libraries/Flickr; King, Charles Bird/Lehman & Duval Lithrs/SMU Central University Libraries/Flickr; SMU Central University Libraries/Flickr), Flickr (Ralph Daily), Getty Images (Marilyn Angel Wynn), iStockphoto (busypix, ChuckSchugPhotography, Юлия Моисеенко), Shutterstock (Everett Historical, Miloje, Emre Tarimcioglu)

Library of Congress Cataloging-in-Publication Data
Names: Bodden, Valerie, author.
Title: Shawnee / Valerie Bodden.
Series: First peoples.
Includes bibliographical references and index.
Summary: An introduction to the Shawnee lifestyle and history, including their forced relocation and how they keep traditions alive today. A Shawnee story recounts the importance of family.
Identifiers:
ISBN 978-1-64026-228-7 (hardcover)
ISBN 978-1-62832-791-5 (pbk)
ISBN 978-1-64000-363-7 (eBook)
This title has been submitted for CIP processing under LCCN 2019938368.
CCSS: RI.1.1, 2, 3, 4, 5, 6, 7; RI.2.1, 2, 3, 4, 5, 6; RI.3.1, 2, 3, 5; RF.1.1, 3, 4; RF.2.3, 4

First Edition HC 9 8 7 6 5 4 3 2 1
First Edition PBK 9 8 7 6 5 4 3 2 1

TABLE *of* CONTENTS

EASTERN PEOPLE

The Shawnee lived in the eastern United States. The name *Shawnee* came from a word that meant "southerners." This is because the Shawnee lived south of other people who spoke similar languages.

The Shawnee were always surrounded by thick forests and water sources.

The Shawnee lived in villages. Each village was led by two chiefs. The peace chief led in times of peace. The war chief ruled during wars.

 In addition to chiefs (above), each village also had a religious leader (left), known as a shaman.

SHAWNEE LIFE

Each Shawnee family lived in a wigwam. Wigwams were made of small poles. The poles were covered with bark or animal skins.

Shawnee hunting parties built smaller, domed wigwams during lengthy hunts.

In the winter, the Shawnee left their villages to hunt. The men hunted elk, deer, and bears. Shawnee men fought in wars, too. They carried clubs and bows and arrows.

The Shawnee traded furs and hides for glass beads, ribbons, metal objects, and guns.

In the spring and summer, Shawnee women farmed. They planted beans, squash, and pumpkins. They gathered wild fruits and nuts. Women also made clothes from deerskin.

Most Shawnee clothing included beadwork or feathered decorations.

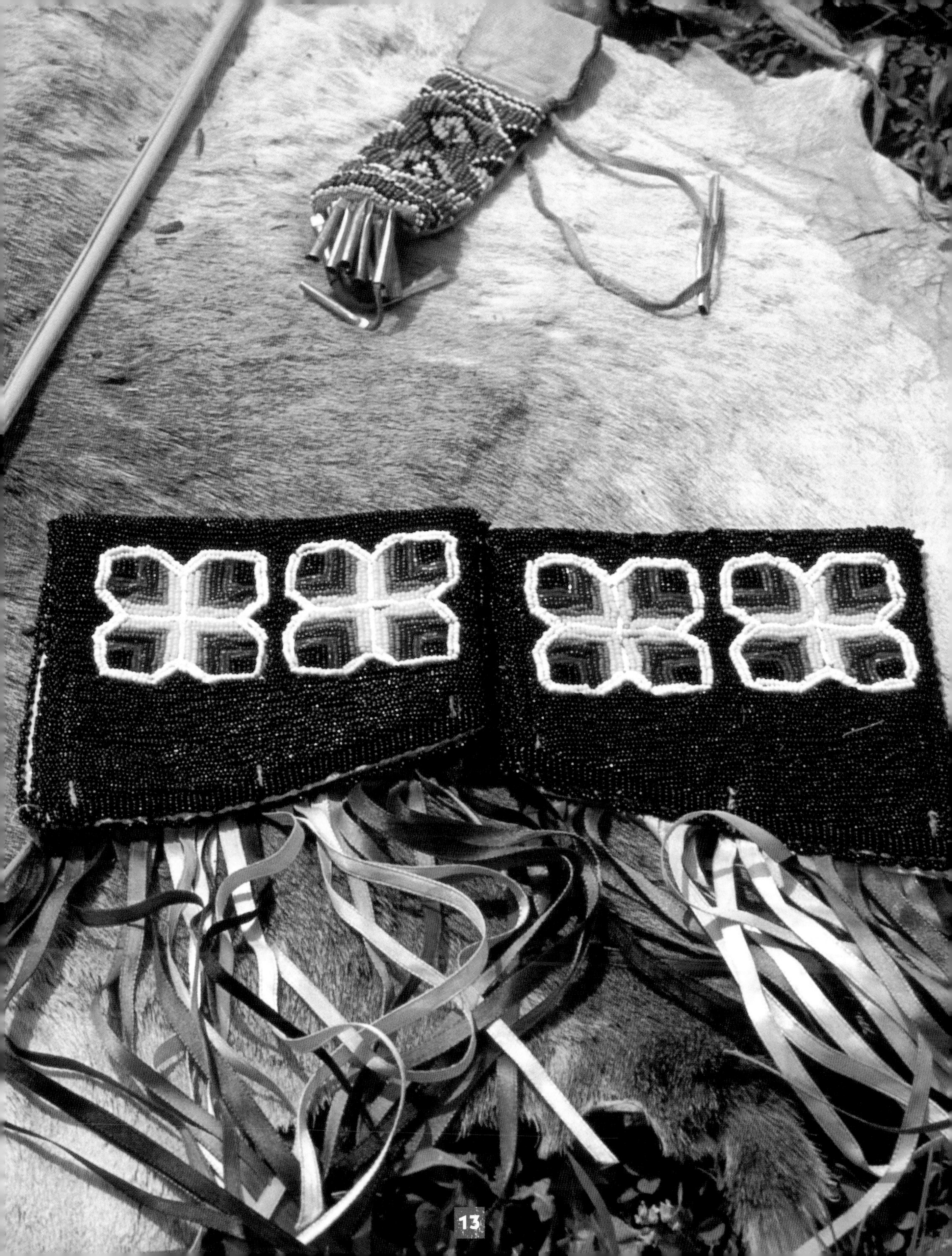

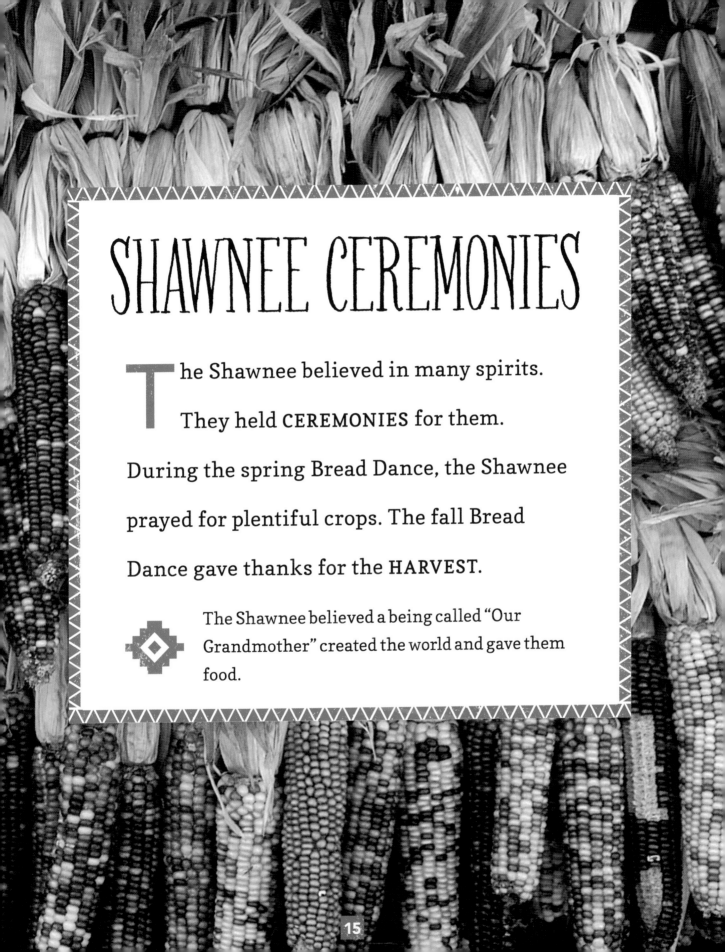

SHAWNEE CEREMONIES

The Shawnee believed in many spirits. They held CEREMONIES for them. During the spring Bread Dance, the Shawnee prayed for plentiful crops. The fall Bread Dance gave thanks for the HARVEST.

◆ The Shawnee believed a being called "Our Grandmother" created the world and gave them food.

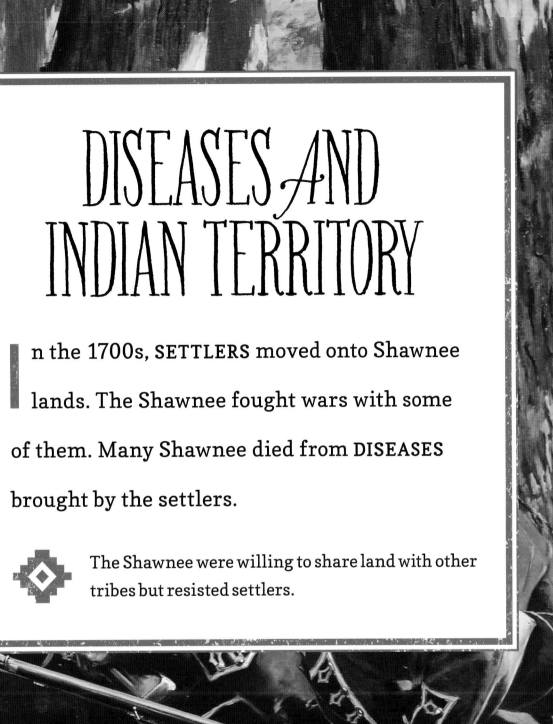

DISEASES AND INDIAN TERRITORY

I n the 1700s, SETTLERS moved onto Shawnee lands. The Shawnee fought wars with some of them. Many Shawnee died from DISEASES brought by the settlers.

The Shawnee were willing to share land with other tribes but resisted settlers.

In the 1800s, the Shawnee were forced to move to **INDIAN TERRITORY**. They lived on reservations there. These were areas of land set aside for American Indians.

The Shawnee were first moved to Ohio before being pushed toward Indian Territory.

BEING SHAWNEE

Today, most Shawnee live in Oklahoma. Some farm or raise cattle. Not many speak the Shawnee language. But some are learning it. They want to keep their TRADITIONS alive.

 Shawnee celebrate their history through artwork, clothing, dances, and drum circles.

A SHAWNEE STORY

The Shawnee told stories to explain the world. In one, a young man saw a basket float down from the sky. He fell in love with a young woman who got out of it. They got married and had a baby. But the woman's home was in the sky. She took the baby there. The man missed them. So he got them all hawk feathers. They became hawks. They still fly above the trees today.

GLOSSARY

CEREMONIES ⇻ special acts carried out according to set rules

DISEASES ⇻ sicknesses

HARVEST ⇻ the crops that have been gathered

INDIAN TERRITORY ⇻ part of the United States that was set aside for American Indians; it is now the state of Oklahoma

SETTLERS ⇻ people who come to live in a new area

TRADITIONS ⇻ beliefs, stories, or ways of doing things that are passed down from parents to their children

READ MORE

Fullman, Joe. *Native North Americans: Dress, Eat, Write, and Play Just Like the Native Americans*. Mankato, Minn.: QEB, 2010.

Morris, Ting. *Arts and Crafts of the Native Americans*. North Mankato, Minn.: Smart Apple Media, 2007.

WEBSITES

Eastern Shawnee Tribe of Oklahoma: Shawnee Language
https://www.estoo-nsn.gov/culture/shawnee-language/
Learn how to say some words in the Shawnee language.

U.S. National Park Service: Tecumseh
https://www.nps.gov/people/tecumseh.htm
Learn more about famous Shawnee chief Tecumseh.

Note: Every effort has been made to ensure that the websites listed above are suitable for children, that they have educational value, and that they contain no inappropriate material. However, because of the nature of the Internet, it is impossible to guarantee that these sites will remain active indefinitely or that their contents will not be altered.

INDEX